THE INSIGNIFICANT ELEPHANT

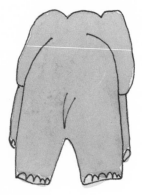

Carol Greene

THE INSIGNIFICANT ELEPHANT

Illustrated by Susan Gantner

Harcourt Brace Jovanovich, Publishers   San Diego   New York   London

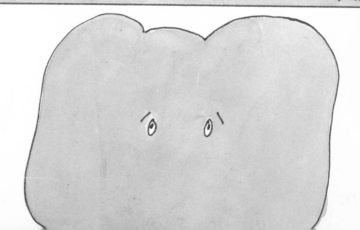

Requests for permission to make copies of any part of the work should be mailed
to: Permissions, Harcourt Brace Jovanovich, Publishers, Orlando, Florida 32887

The illustrations were done in watercolor plus pen-and-ink.
The text and display were set on the Linotron 202 in Della Robbia,
composed by Thompson Type, San Diego, California.
Separations were made by Heinz Weber, Inc., Los Angeles, California.
Printed by Rae Publishing Co., Inc., Cedar Grove, New Jersey.
Bound by A. Horowitz & Son, Fairfield, New Jersey.
Production by Virginia R. Anson.
Designed by Joy Chu.

Library of Congress Cataloging in Publication Data
Greene, Carol.
The insignificant elephant.
Summary: An elephant nobody ever notices turns his
appearance to the kingdom's advantage when he becomes
chief spy and a hero as well.
1. Children's stories, American.   [1. Elephants—
Fiction]   I. Gantner, Susan, ill.   II. Title
PZ7.G82845In 1985   [E]   84-15831
ISBN 0-15-238730-7

Printed in the United States of America
First edition
A B C D E

For Caryn Elizabeth Greene
—C. G.—

To Mother and Dad
—S. G.—

No one noticed Humber, and that was very strange, because Humber was an elephant. He lived with a herd of other elephants in the Royal Coconut Grove around the Pearlish Palace of the Proud Pasha Pusha of Rabbidum. Everyone noticed the other elephants, fine fat creatures that they were.

But no one noticed Humber. He was an insignificant elephant, and that is not an easy thing to be.

One day, the Head of the Pearlish Palace
Guards paid a visit to the Royal Coconut Grove.
He waved his spear and stamped his feet to show
how fierce he was. But he looked worried.

"We have heard," he said, "that the dread Januaries plan to harm our Proud Pasha Pusha. But we don't know what they have in mind. We need a spy to find out. Are there any volunteers?"

"I think not," said the oldest elephant.

"Hardly," said another.

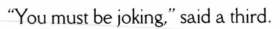

"You must be joking," said a third.

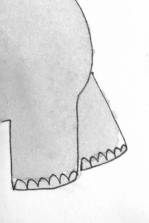

One by one, the elephants shook their heads and lumbered off — all except Humber. But no one had noticed he was there in the first place.

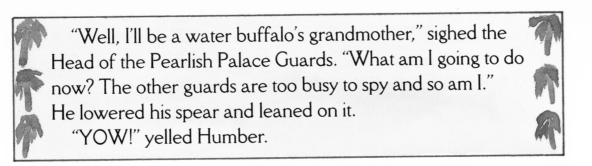

"Well, I'll be a water buffalo's grandmother," sighed the Head of the Pearlish Palace Guards. "What am I going to do now? The other guards are too busy to spy and so am I."
He lowered his spear and leaned on it.

"YOW!" yelled Humber.

"I beg your pardon," said the Head. "I didn't notice you."

"That's quite all right," said Humber. "No one ever does."

"Oh, they don't, don't they?" said the Head. "Then you're the one! What could be better than a spy no one notices? You're hired. Good luck!"

And in no time at all, Humber found himself on the road to the land of the dread Januaries.

It was a long and dangerous trip to the land of the dread Januaries.

There were footpads and highwaypersons, landslides and blizzards, and even a tiger or two.

But Humber used his wits and, sure enough, no one noticed him.

Finally, he reached the January Gates, where he cleverly disguised himself as a sack of mail. He was delivered immediately — straight to the Pepperpot Palace of the Grand Poopah of January.

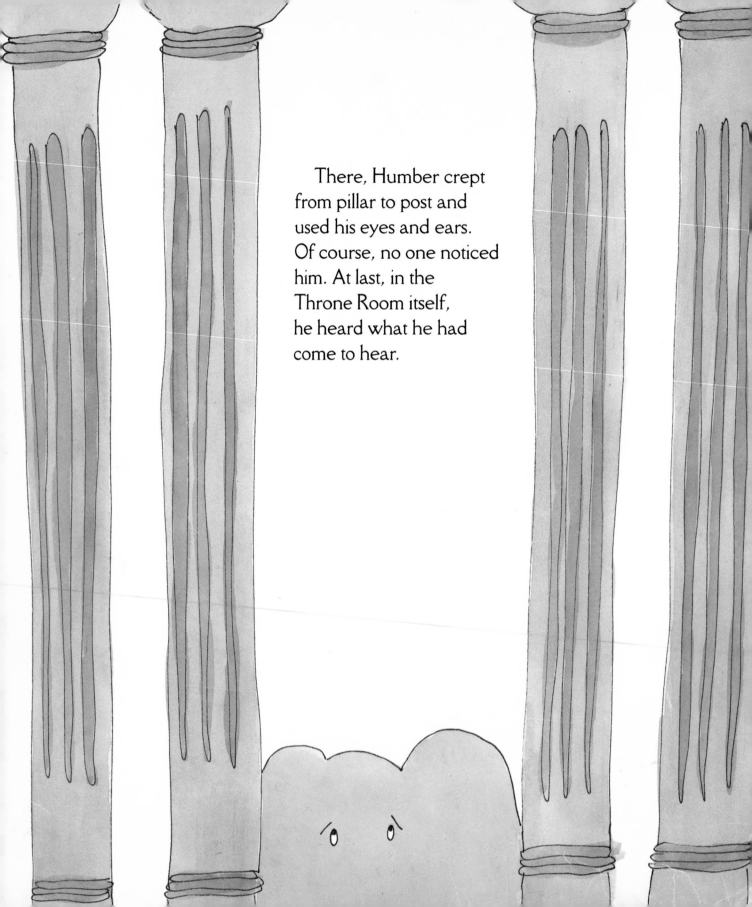

There, Humber crept
from pillar to post and
used his eyes and ears.
Of course, no one noticed
him. At last, in the
Throne Room itself,
he heard what he had
come to hear.

"The helicopters are almost ready,"
said the Grand Poopah to the Grand
Poopina. "Tomorrow night they will fly to
Rabbidum. They will hover over the Royal
Coconut Grove and my dread Januaries will
steal every last coconut. The Proud Pasha Pusha
will be *humiliated.*"

"He certainly will, dear," said the Grand Poopina.
"He will be furious, too. His cooks use those coconuts
to make his favorite coconut stew. I can hardly wait
until tomorrow night."

I must hurry, thought Humber.
There is no time to lose.

He dashed out of the Pepperpot
Palace, through the January Gates,
past the tigers and landslides and
blizzards, past the footpads and
highwaypersons, and back to
Rabbidum.

He got there early the next morning.

"Listen! Listen!" he panted as he skidded into the Pearlish Palace. "I have important news."

"Did you hear something?" the Head of the Pearlish Palace Guards asked his assistant.

"I don't think so," said the assistant.

"Maybe there is a mosquito in here," said the Head.

"Maybe," said his assistant.

This calls for desperate action, thought Humber. So he cleverly disguised himself as a telephone and rang. When the Head answered him, Humber told him about the helicopters.

"Mercy!" cried the Head. "What shall we do?"

"Don't worry," said Humber. "I have a plan."

The Head of the Pearlish Palace
Guards did not want to try Humber's
plan. He thought it was silly. But he
could not think of a better one. So that
evening he went to the Royal Coconut
Grove and ordered all the elephants
to sleep in the coconut trees.

"I *beg* your pardon!" said the oldest elephant.

"Surely you jest," said another.

"I mean, *really!*" said a third.

"You heard me," said the Head. He waved his spear and stamped his feet to show how fierce he was. "Now, march!"

So, one after another, the elephants climbed the trees and tried to go to sleep. It was not easy.

Humber climbed the tallest tree so he could keep watch. Finally, at midnight, he heard the helicopters, buzzing and sputtering like a swarm of noisy gnats.

"Wake up!" he yelled. "They're almost here!"

But the other elephants didn't notice him. They went right on sleeping.

This calls for desperate action, thought Humber. So he cleverly disguised himself as an alarm clock and rang. The other elephants woke up at once.

"The dread Januaries are almost here," Humber told them. "This is what we must do."

A moment later, the helicopters swooped low over the Royal Coconut Grove. At once each of the elephants took a deep, deep breath — and blew. *Whoosh!*

The helicopters did not have a chance. They were blown all the way back to the land of the dread Januaries.

The Grand Poopah and the Grand Poopina were humiliated.

And Humber was a hero.

The next morning, the Proud Pasha Pusha himself came to the Royal Coconut Grove to meet Humber.

"Where is he?" asked the Proud Pasha Pusha.
"Right here, your Proudship," said Humber.
"Humber is rather insignificant, you see,"
explained the Head of the Pearlish Palace Guards.

"Not anymore," said the Proud Pasha Pusha. He fastened a huge medal on Humber. *For significant, valorous, and smart service in defense of Proud Pasha Pusha and country,* it read.

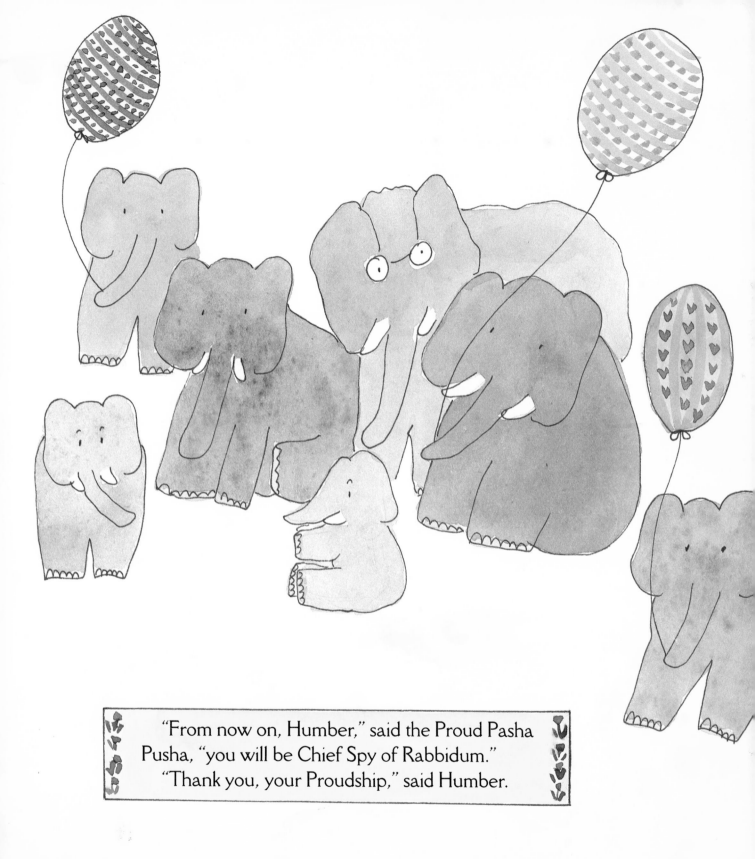

"From now on, Humber," said the Proud Pasha Pusha, "you will be Chief Spy of Rabbidum."
"Thank you, your Proudship," said Humber.

Humber's medal was so big that no one could miss it. From that day on, he wore it all the time — except when he did not want to be noticed.